The Boxcar Children Mysteries

THE BOXCAR CHILDREN
SURPRISE ISLAND
THE YELLOW HOUSE MYSTERY
MYSTERY RANCH
MIKE'S MYSTERY
BLUE BAY MYSTERY
THE WOODSHED MYSTERY
THE LIGHTHOUSE MYSTERY
MOUNTAIN TOP MYSTERY
SCHOOLHOUSE MYSTERY
CABOOSE MYSTERY
HOUSEBOAT MYSTERY
SNOWBOUND MYSTERY
TREE HOUSE MYSTERY
BICYCLE MYSTERY
MYSTERY IN THE SAND
MYSTERY BEHIND THE WALL
BUS STATION MYSTERY
BENNY UNCOVERS A MYSTERY
THE HAUNTED CABIN
  MYSTERY
THE DESERTED LIBRARY
  MYSTERY
THE ANIMAL SHELTER
  MYSTERY
THE OLD MOTEL MYSTERY
THE MYSTERY OF THE HIDDEN
  PAINTING
THE AMUSEMENT PARK
  MYSTERY
THE MYSTERY OF THE MIXED-
  UP ZOO

THE CAMP-OUT MYSTERY
THE MYSTERY GIRL
THE MYSTERY CRUISE
THE DISAPPEARING FRIEND
  MYSTERY
THE MYSTERY OF THE SINGING
  GHOST
MYSTERY IN THE SNOW
THE PIZZA MYSTERY
THE MYSTERY HORSE
THE MYSTERY AT THE DOG
  SHOW
THE CASTLE MYSTERY
THE MYSTERY OF THE LOST
  VILLAGE
THE MYSTERY ON THE ICE
THE MYSTERY OF THE
  PURPLE POOL
THE GHOST SHIP MYSTERY
THE MYSTERY IN
  WASHINGTON, DC
THE CANOE TRIP MYSTERY
THE MYSTERY OF THE HIDDEN
  BEACH
THE MYSTERY OF THE MISSING
  CAT
THE MYSTERY AT SNOWFLAKE
  INN
THE MYSTERY ON STAGE
THE DINOSAUR MYSTERY
THE MYSTERY OF THE STOLEN
  MUSIC

THE MYSTERY AT THE BALL PARK

THE CHOCOLATE SUNDAE MYSTERY

THE MYSTERY OF THE HOT AIR BALLOON

THE MYSTERY BOOKSTORE

THE PILGRIM VILLAGE MYSTERY

THE MYSTERY OF THE STOLEN BOXCAR

MYSTERY IN THE CAVE

THE MYSTERY ON THE TRAIN

THE MYSTERY AT THE FAIR

THE MYSTERY OF THE LOST MINE

THE GUIDE DOG MYSTERY

THE HURRICANE MYSTERY

THE PET SHOP MYSTERY

THE MYSTERY OF THE SECRET MESSAGE

THE FIREHOUSE MYSTERY

THE MYSTERY IN SAN FRANCISCO

THE NIAGARA FALLS MYSTERY

THE MYSTERY AT THE ALAMO

THE OUTER SPACE MYSTERY

THE SOCCER MYSTERY

THE MYSTERY IN THE OLD ATTIC

THE GROWLING BEAR MYSTERY

THE MYSTERY OF THE LAKE MONSTER

THE MYSTERY AT PEACOCK HALL

THE WINDY CITY MYSTERY

THE BLACK PEARL MYSTERY

THE CEREAL BOX MYSTERY

THE PANTHER MYSTERY

THE MYSTERY OF THE QUEEN'S JEWELS

THE STOLEN SWORD MYSTERY

THE BASKETBALL MYSTERY

THE MOVIE STAR MYSTERY

THE MYSTERY OF THE BLACK RAVEN

THE MYSTERY OF THE PIRATE'S MAP

THE MYSTERY OF THE PIRATE'S MAP

created by
GERTRUDE CHANDLER WARNER

Illustrated by Charles Tang

ALBERT WHITMAN & Company
Morton Grove, Illinois

ISBN 0-8075-5454-5

7 9 10 8 6

Printed in the U.S.A.

Contents

CHAPTER   PAGE

1. Benny's Discovery   1
2. The Legend of John Finney's
   Treasure   13
3. Benny Becomes Famous   22
4. Lots of Stairs and Millionaires   38
5. An Unwelcome Visitor   50
6. Danger, Danger, Everywhere!   60
7. The Helpful Mr. Ford   76
8. The Final Offer   88
9. What You See Is What You Get   96
10. Good News All Around   114

CHAPTER 1

Benny's Discovery

It seemed like an ideal afternoon for a walk on the beach. The sky was blue, the breeze was warm, and the ocean was calm and peaceful. The only thing that kept it from being perfect was the mess the storm had left behind.

"Yuck, more seaweed!" six-year-old Benny Alden said as he stepped over another ragged green pile of it. Watch, the Aldens' dog, tagged along behind Benny.

"And more of these little black shells, broken open," ten-year-old Violet added.

She picked one up between her thumb and forefinger. "What are they, anyway?"

"I think they're called mussels," Jessie said. She was twelve years old and had long brown hair. "I'll bet the seagulls are happy they're here. Now they've got plenty to eat."

Benny smiled. "There's nothing wrong with that!" he said. The others laughed. Benny had a very healthy appetite.

"Tom would know what they are," Jessie continued. "He knows a lot about this area."

Tom was Tom Harrison, a retired elementary school teacher and an old friend of the children's grandfather. He owned and ran a bed-and-breakfast a few blocks inland, and he had invited the Aldens to visit for a week. Grandfather hadn't seen him in years, and the children were thrilled at the idea of spending some time along the shore. So Grandfather cheerfully accepted his old friend's invitation. The two men were back at the house now, catching up on old times.

"The storm must've been pretty bad,"

Henry commented, walking behind everyone else. He was tall and thin, and at fourteen he was the oldest child. His full name was Henry James Alden. He was named after his grandfather, James Henry Alden. "I guess that's why there are hardly any sunbathers here today. There's no place to lie down."

There were all sorts of things from the sea scattered on the beach: thousands of broken shells, small stones, seaweed clumps, and chunks of rotting driftwood. Tom had mentioned that storms were common along the shore. This one had hit the night before the Aldens arrived.

"Oooh! Here's a pretty one!" Violet said excitedly. She crouched down and picked up a perfectly formed shell. Then she put it in the plastic bag she had brought along.

"Do you think you have enough yet?" Jessie asked.

"Hmm . . . almost," Violet replied. She had offered to make seashell necklaces for everyone, and now the children were searching for all the perfect shells they could find. Violet was always doing artistic things. She liked to draw and usually brought a pad and coloring pencils with her whenever the Aldens traveled. Her favorite color was, of course, violet.

The Alden children lived with their grandfather in a large and beautiful house back in Greenfield, Connecticut. But there was a time when an abandoned boxcar was their home. After their parents died, they had no place to live. Then they discovered the old train car in the woods. While they were living in it, their grandfather came looking for them. They hid from him, thinking that he was mean. But they soon found out that he wasn't mean at all.

He took them back to Greenfield and brought the boxcar, too. He put it in the backyard so the children could visit it anytime they wished.

Although there weren't many sunbathers on the beach, there were other people walking around. A few were wearing headphones and carrying metal detectors. Benny had been watching them for a while. As one man knelt down and dug into the sand, Benny asked, "What is that man doing?"

A stranger's voice answered, "He's looking for buried treasure!"

Benny said, "Buried treasure? You mean like gold or something?"

The man shrugged. "Gold, silver, whatever."

"And what are those things you both have?" Benny asked.

"Metal detectors," Henry answered, "I think. . . ."

"That's right," the man answered, and gave Benny a smile. "It's called a metal detector because . . . well, because it detects metal."

"That means it finds metal, right?" Jessie asked.

"Yep. You wave it back and forth just above the ground, and if there's anything made of metal under the sand" — he tapped his headphones — "you hear a beeping sound in here."

Benny looked around the beach at the other people who had metal detectors.

"Have you found anything today?" he asked.

The man reached into his pocket and produced two silver coins.

"Do you think they've been here for a long time?" Henry asked.

The man nodded. "Probably."

"Then how come no one else with a metal detector found them before today?"

"The storm," the man answered. "Whenever there's a big storm, new things always show up, things that may have been buried too deep for the metal detectors to pick up before. It happens all the time. That's why all the metal-detector people are out today. This is the best kind of day to find stuff."

Benny's eyes twinkled. "Boy, I sure hope I find some old coins!"

The man laughed. "You might; you never know. You just have to keep your eyes open and pay attention as you walk."

He took another drink from his water bottle. "Well, I've got to get back to work. Who knows what other little treasures are lying underground, just waiting for someone like me to find them? Good luck."

"You, too," the children said, and the man walked off.

"Oh, boy, old coins!" Benny squealed as they all went back to their seashell search. Suddenly the sand was ten times more interesting to him.

Violet and Jessie both found a few more shells. Henry didn't have quite as much luck. And Benny, off by himself a few yards from the others, kept a close watch for anything that looked like it was made of metal. Shells were suddenly the last thing on his mind.

As he walked around the side of one particularly large rock, something round and shiny caught his attention. He reached down and grabbed it. Then his shoulders slumped with disappointment — it was nothing more than an old bottle cap. He stuffed it into the pocket of his shorts so he could throw it into a garbage can when he got back to the boardwalk.

He was just about to turn away when something else caught his eye. It wasn't round and shiny like an old coin, but it still looked interesting. It barely stuck out of the sand and was hiding in the dark space between two huge rocks.

He dropped to his knees and began digging.

"Benny, what are you up to?" Henry asked curiously.

"I'm digging."

"Digging what?"

"I don't know. It feels like it's made of . . . of glass."

"Glass?" Jessie said, slightly alarmed. She was always watching out for her brothers and sister. Although she was only twelve years old, sometimes she acted and sounded much older. "Be careful, Benny. It might be broken. You could cut yourself."

"Maybe you shouldn't —" Henry started to say, then Benny suddenly rolled backward. His prize was in his hand.

It was a bottle.

"Oh, my goodness!" Violet gasped.

"Wow," Henry said softly.

"Look how old it is!" Jessie exclaimed.

What Jessie said was definitely true — the bottle was very, very old. It didn't have a nice, neat shape like the bottles the children were used to seeing. And it was sealed shut, but not by a cap. Instead there was a rotting cork stopper in the hole.

"Let me see," Henry said, kneeling down next to his brother. Benny handed it to him without taking his eyes off it.

"Hmmm," he said thoughtfully, wiping away the sand. "Looks pretty old. I'll bet this thing is —"

Then Henry stopped talking, and the others stopped moving. They all saw it at the same time. . . .

There was a piece of paper inside.

"Wow," Henry said again. "Look at that!"

Benny got up and brushed himself off. He took the bottle back and looked closely at the piece of paper inside. It had turned brown and was cracked around the edges.

"What do you think it is?" he asked.

"I don't know, but we'll have to take out whatever's in the neck to get it," Henry said.

"Can we go back to the house now?" Benny asked excitedly.

"Sure," Henry answered, "let's go."

The Aldens began walking back, with Benny in the lead. He was skipping along happily with the bottle in hand.

Just before they reached the boardwalk, a woman holding a camera came up to them. She was dressed in long pants and a dark overcoat. This seemed strange to the children because it was such a hot day, but no one said anything.

"What have you found there, young man?" she said to Benny. Her voice was very loud. "I noticed you digging over by the rocks!"

"Ummm . . . I found a bottle," Benny told her, holding it up.

"Wow, that looks like an old one!" the woman said. "Can I take a picture of it?"

Before anyone had a chance to answer, the woman pulled the camera to her face and clicked off two shots.

"I like to take pictures around the beach," she told them. "I don't sell many, but I'd like to. There are lots of pretty things to photograph around here!"

Then she turned and hurried away.

The Aldens looked at one another. Jessie said, "She seemed a little strange."

"You're right," Henry agreed. "Well, let's get back and see what's inside the bottle."

CHAPTER 2

The Legend of John Finney's Treasure

Tom's bed-and-breakfast, which also happened to be the house in which he lived, was very large and very old. It sat on a sunny, tree-lined street a few blocks from the beach. A painted sign near the sidewalk said, THE SEA BREEZE MANOR, ESTABLISHED 1919. ALL ARE WELCOME.

The children went up the walk with Benny still in the lead. Then they went into the lobby and shut the door quietly behind them. Henry tapped the little silver bell on the counter. A moment later a man appeared from behind a curtain. He was small and roundish, and he had a full head of white hair. The children's grandfather was right behind him.

"Hello, kids!" Tom said. He had a wonderful smile, and it matched his sweet and jolly personality. He was everybody's friend, and he loved people. He told the children that this was the main reason he had bought the bed-and-breakfast. He got to meet new and interesting people all the time.

"Did you all have a good time at the beach?" he asked.

"We sure did," Henry replied.

"Did you find enough shells for your necklaces, Violet?" Grandfather asked.

Violet held up the bag. "I might be a few short, but I can always go back."

"Shells weren't the only thing we found," Henry added.

"Oh?" said Grandfather.

"Benny found something, too. Show them, Benny."

"Look at this!" he said proudly, holding up the bottle.

The two men leaned over the counter to have a look. Tom pushed his glasses up. "Wow, that's a really old one!" he said.

"Where did you find it, Benny?" Grandfather asked.

"It was between two big rocks. Only the top of it was sticking out. And look at this!" Benny said. He turned the bottle so Tom and Grandfather could see the little piece of paper curled up inside.

"What's that?" Tom asked.

"It's a small piece of paper," Jessie answered, "but we have to get the bottle open to see what's written on it."

Grandfather took the bottle from Benny and looked at it. "The cork is so old that it would probably break if I tried to pull it. But I'll bet I could grind it out with a screwdriver."

"I'll go get one," Tom told him.

After Tom brought back the screwdriver, Grandfather pulled a lamp over to a nearby table and sat down. The others gathered around him. He stuck the head of the screwdriver into the neck of the bottle and began grinding out the cork. It was so old and dry that it broke apart easily. Once the neck tube was clear, Tom brought over a long pair of tweezers from his desk.

"I used to use these when I built ship models inside bottles," he told everyone.

"Oh, so that's how that's done," Violet said. She thought someday she'd like to try that.

Slowly and carefully Grandfather brought out the old piece of paper. Once it was on the table, he turned on the reading lamp, which was very bright. The children moved in closer. Then Grandfather gently unrolled the paper, and everyone gasped.

The paper had turned dark brown over the years, but the drawings on it were still clear. There were some trees, a few rocks, and some squiggly lines that seemed to imply water.

But it was the dotted line that grabbed everyone's attention. It started at the top of

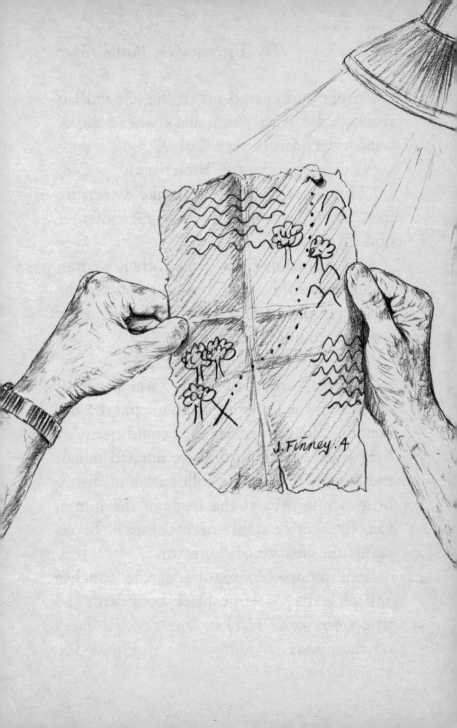

the paper and curved off to the left until it reached the trees. And that's where the X was. A very large, very dark X.

"Oh, my goodness!" Violet said.

"This looks like . . . well, like a treasure map, or at least part of one," Grandfather said. "And what's this here?"

In the bottom right-hand corner, written in letters so tiny that it almost couldn't be seen, was the name "J. Finney." Next to it was the number "4."

"J. Finney. Who's that?"

All eyes turned to Tom. "You know, it does sound a little bit familiar, but I can't really —Hey! I wonder if it could be . . ."

His voice trailed off as he hurried out of the room. The others followed him into a little sitting area at the front of the house. On the coffee table were several books about the history of the town.

Tom plopped onto one of the couches and picked up a large black book with the title *Cherrystone Harbor, Yesterday and Today* on the cover.

"If I remember right, there was a little story in here about — yes! Here it is!"

He put the book flat on his knees so everyone could see. On the left-hand page was the heading "John Finney." Underneath were a few paragraphs of text. On the other page was a painting of Finney. He was standing on the deck of his ship with his hands on his hips. His long hair was as black as night, as was his tangled mustache. His eyes looked mean, but his mouth was curved in a smile.

Tom handed the book over to Violet and said, "Why don't you read it for us, young lady?"

Taking the book onto her own lap, Violet smiled and swept her hair back behind her ears. " 'John Alexander Finney was one of the most colorful and eccentric pirates who ever sailed the high seas,' " she began.

Benny's eyes widened. "Wow! A real pirate!"

Violet continued, " 'He was the captain of his very first ship when he was only nineteen years old, and by the time he was twenty-five he had sailed halfway around the world. He was best known for his wild behavior. He and his men would dock at any port that caught their fancy and go inland for days, causing all sorts of trouble. Like all pirates, John was not only a sailor but also a thief. During his lifetime he stole hundreds of thousands, maybe even millions, of dollars' worth of gold, silver, and jewelry.

" 'When he got older, he decided to hide all the treasure he'd stolen over the years. Then he drew a map that showed its exact location. But he didn't want anyone to find it too easily, so, during his last sailing journey, he cut the map into four pieces and hid each piece in a different part of the world. Over the years, three of the four pieces have been recovered, but the fourth has yet to turn up. It is known that John Finney stopped in Cherrystone on his famous final voyage, so it is possible that he hid the fourth and final piece here during that visit. But so far no one has found it. And this piece is by far the most interesting, because . . .' "

"What's it say, Violet?" Jessie squealed. "Don't keep us in suspense!"

Violet looked up. " '. . . because very near the last piece of the map, so says the legend, lies the treasure.' "

CHAPTER 3

Benny Becomes Famous

After a night of dreams about John Finney's treasure, the Alden children awoke to breakfast on Tom's front porch. Jessie and Violet both chose fresh fruit and toasted bagels. Benny chose his favorite, cereal and milk. Henry had scrambled eggs and crisp bacon. But the food went down slowly because the children were too busy talking about what they were going to do after they found the treasure.

"I'm going to buy my own pizza parlor!"

Benny told his siblings. "Then I can have all the pizza I want!"

"I'm going to get more art supplies," Violet said. "And then I'll take some classes so I can draw better pictures."

"What's wrong with the ones you make now?" Benny asked.

Violet smiled.

"What would you do, Jessie?" asked Henry.

"I don't know. I'd probably just give the money to Grandfather. He's done so much for us."

The other children nodded. That did sound like a perfect idea.

Grandfather came onto the porch at that moment, followed by Tom. They both had their plates with them.

"So what's the plan for today?" Tom asked as he took his seat and jabbed a fork into his eggs.

"We're going to start at the local library," Henry told him. The others nodded. This was what they had decided last night, just before they went to bed. "Maybe we can find information about the other pieces of the map. Once we know what the other three pieces look like, we can start hunting for the treasure."

"Sounds good," Tom said. "This should be fun for you kids."

"We love mysteries!" Benny said enthusiastically.

"So I've heard. You've solved quite a few, haven't you?" asked Tom.

"Yes, sir. Lots of them," Benny replied.

"Well, don't forget about the beach. I heard on the radio this morning that the water's supposed to be warm all week," said Tom.

Grandfather took a sip of his orange juice, then said, "You know, I was thinking about something last night. Something about this treasure."

"What's that, Grandfather?" Jessie asked.

"It might be best if you didn't mention it to anyone. I know it's exciting and everything, but you should keep it to yourselves."

The children looked at one another in confusion. "Why?" Jessie asked.

"Because I'm sure a lot of other people would love to get their hands on the last piece of the map. Remember, John Finney's treasure is probably worth a fortune, and there are plenty of people who would love to find it. With the help of that piece, a person could become very, very rich."

"But we're not trying to get rich, Grandfather," Violet explained. "We just want to have fun *looking* for the treasure."

"Solving the mystery!" Benny reminded them.

"I know that, children," Grandfather replied. "But there are other people who want the treasure only so they can get rich."

"And some of them will do almost *anything* to get it," Tom added.

"Are we in any kind of danger?" Benny asked.

"No, not as long as no one else knows," Grandfather assured them. "You haven't told anyone else, right?"

Henry answered for all of them. "No, we haven't said anything to anybody."

They all went back to their meals, and Henry went back inside to get more juice.

Then Jessie suddenly cried out, "The photographer!"

Tom was so surprised by this that he dropped his fork in his lap. "What?"

"The photographer!" Jessie said again. "Remember, Violet? The lady at the beach as we were leaving?"

"Oh, yes," Violet said. "I do remember."

"What are you talking about?" Tom asked.

"A lady with a camera took a picture of the bottle," Jessie said.

"Really?" Grandfather asked.

"I think she was just walking around, taking pictures," Violet offered. "It was a pretty day."

Tom nodded. "Oh, sure, a lot of people do that when they come here."

"Is it something we should worry about?" Jessie asked.

"I don't think so," Tom told her. Then he

asked, "But aside from this lady photographer, no one else knows?"

"No," Jessie said. "No one. I'm sure of it."

"If we're lucky, maybe we'll find pictures of the other three pieces today," Violet said. "Then we can go looking for the treasure before we head back to Greenfield."

Out on the sidewalk, a young girl came along on a bicycle. A canvas pouch was tied to the handlebars. She reached into it and pulled out a newspaper with a rubber band wrapped around it, which she then threw onto the front step.

Violet opened the door and picked up the paper. The color picture on the front page caught her attention right away.

"Oh, no . . ." she whispered.

Everyone turned. "What, Violet? What's the matter?"

She pulled the rubber band off the paper and unfolded it so everyone could see. "Look at this!"

Right on page one was a photograph of Benny proudly holding up his bottle. And the headline underneath, in huge letters, screamed, COULD THIS BE THE MISSING PIECE TO JOHN FINNEY'S PUZZLE?

Tom jumped out of his seat. He looked at the picture closely, then turned the newspaper sideways to read the name of the photographer. It was written in very small print up the left side.

"Oh, no wonder . . ." he muttered.

"No wonder what, Tom?" Grandfather asked.

"Meredith Baker," Tom said.

"Who's that?" Violet asked.

"She's a local lady. Everyone knows her. Of all the people who had to be there when Benny found the bottle . . ." Tom said.

"What do you mean?" Jessie asked.

"She's very nosy, very chatty, and she's always looking for something to do. As soon as she got the picture developed, she probably went right to the newspaper. A lot of people around here know that this is one of the places John Finney's treasure might be buried. I'm sure the newspaper reporters figured it out right away." Tom sighed and looked at Benny. "Well, so much for keeping it a secret."

The secret of Benny's discovery was out now, and nothing could be done about it, so the children went to the town library as planned. They walked in and went straight to the information desk. The woman who was working there, a younger lady with dark hair and glasses, smiled at them. "Is there anything I can help you with today?"

"We're looking for a book on buried treasures," Jessie said carefully. She didn't want to say too much.

"Well, our computer catalog is right over there," the woman said, pointing to a long table in the middle of the room with a row of computers on it. "Just follow the directions on the screen. It's easy; you'll see."

"Thank you," Jessie replied.

The librarian had been right — the computer catalog system was very easy to use. The children decided to do a subject search for any books about treasures and treasure hunting. There turned out to be eight titles

available. As Jessie called out the Dewey
decimal numbers, Henry wrote them down
on a piece of scrap paper. The library help-
fully supplied a small pile of scrap paper and
a cupful of pencils next to each computer.

The children went to find the books, and
it took them only a few minutes. Henry and
Jessie immediately began searching through
the index of each one to see if John Finney's
treasure was mentioned.

Violet said, "I'm going to browse through
one of the computers for anything else that
might help," then went back to the long
table in the main room.

As she began working her way through
the computer's menus, a man walked into
the library. He looked vaguely familiar to
Violet. He went to the front desk and said,
"Good mornin', Miriam."

The lady who had helped the children
find the treasure books looked up from her
desk, saw the man, and frowned.

"Hello," she said simply. Then she went
back to what she was doing.

"Nice day, isn't it?" the man asked.

"Yes, very nice," Miriam answered.

"Are you gonna go outside and enjoy it?" the man continued.

By the look on Miriam's face, she wasn't the type of person who enjoyed small talk. "No, I'm very busy."

The man laughed. The room was empty except for Violet, and she was trying to pretend she wasn't paying attention. "Doesn't look too busy, miss."

"I'm paid to be here all day," the librarian said firmly, "so it's only fair that I stay here all day."

The man kept quiet for the next few moments, and Violet breathed a sigh of relief. She went back to tapping away on the computer keyboard to continue her search. But a moment later she heard something that made her heart sink —

She looked over and saw the man pick up a copy of that day's newspaper, which had been sitting on the front desk. "Hmmm, what's this?" he said to no one in particular. He studied Benny's picture and read the story underneath with great interest. "John Finney's treasure?" he said with a grin. "That's gotta be worth millions." The man paused for just a moment, then his eyes widened. "Hey!" he said. "I know this kid!" He held the picture up to the librarian. "I saw him just the other day!"

At that moment Violet remembered who the man was, and her stomach rolled over — he was the man they'd talked to on the beach — the one with the metal detector!

The librarian looked up at the picture, and at first she seemed very annoyed that this stranger had once again pulled her attention away from her work. Then she realized who the child in the picture was. "Oh, my goodness," she gasped, "that's — " She pointed in the general direction of the Aldens, then pulled her hand back down, realizing the mistake she had just made.

The man stared at her for a moment, looked in the direction in which she had pointed, then looked back at her. "He's here?" he asked.

"No, I think I made a mistake. Yes, that's it. I made a mistake," she said. But her excuses didn't fool the man, who was already heading around the counter.

Violet hurried back to where the others were. "We've got a problem," she said nervously.

Henry, with a book in his hands, said, "What? What's wrong?"

Violet quickly explained what had happened, turning back every few seconds to make sure the man hadn't found them yet.

"Oh, boy, we've got to get out of here," Henry said. He quickly pieced together a plan. "Okay, here's what we'll do. I've got a book here with some information on the treasure. I don't know how useful it'll be, but it's the only book that has something. It's also got a picture of one of the other map pieces."

"Too bad we can't just read it here," Jessie said. "We could use the copying machine and we wouldn't even need the book."

"Well, maybe we can still get lucky,"

Henry said, then proceeded to explain the rest of the plan.

Benny and Henry were heading toward the door when the man spotted them. "Hey, you!" he barked.

The two boys stopped and turned. "Yes?" Henry asked.

The man hurried over to them. "I'd like to talk to you for a moment."

"Yes, sir?" Benny said.

"I understand you found something on the beach the other day. A piece of an old map?" the man asked.

"Yes, I did," Benny replied. "Hey, I remember you!"

The man smiled. "You do? Good."

While he was asking questions, Jessie and Violet tiptoed over to the front desk.

"I'm really sorry about all of this," the librarian said. "I didn't mean to —"

"It's okay," Jessie whispered. "But we need your help."

"Sure, what?"

Jessie brought the book out from behind her back and set it on the desk.

"Could you copy pages thirty-four through thirty-seven for us?"

The woman smiled. "Of course. Just give me a second."

". . . I didn't know what it was," Benny continued, "so I gave it to the man for five dollars."

"*Five dollars?* Do you have any idea how much that treasure is worth?" the man asked.

"Treasure? What treasure?" asked Benny. He and Henry looked at each other.

"John Fin — er, nothing. What I meant to say was, an old bottle like that must be worth more than five dollars. I meant it was a real treasure. And you gave it away for almost nothing," the man said.

"Not nothing," Benny corrected him, rubbing his stomach and smiling. "I bought five slices of pizza with the money!"

The man slapped himself on the forehead. "Pizza!" he said to the ceiling.

Back at the desk, the librarian reappeared

from the back room with a few sheets of paper. She gave them to Jessie, who quickly folded them and put them into her pocket. Then Jessie took out a dollar bill and offered it to the woman.

"No, don't worry about it. It was the least I could do after causing you all this trouble. Do you still want the book?" she asked.

"No, ma'am," Jessie said, "but we'll put it back on the shelf if you —"

"No need, I'll take care of it." She smiled warmly. "Good luck with your search. I hope you find the treasure."

Jessie and Violet smiled back. "Thanks." They left the library through the back door.

Fifteen minutes later, Henry and Benny met up with Jessie and Violet at an ice-cream parlor around the corner, just as they had planned. Everyone congratulated Benny on fooling the man from the beach into thinking he didn't know anything about the treasure. They all agreed Benny should go into acting when he grew up. He just smiled and slipped another spoonful of chocolate ice cream into his mouth.

CHAPTER 4

Lots of Stairs and Millionaires

"I can't say I'm happy about this," Grandfather said after hearing of his grandchildren's latest experience. They were all back on the porch, enjoying the coolness of the late afternoon.

"Oh, James, they're fine," Tom pointed out, patting Benny on the back. "I think Benny handled the situation brilliantly."

"I didn't like lying to that man," Benny assured his grandfather, "but I wasn't sure what he would do if I told him the truth, that I still had the piece of the map."

Grandfather nodded. "I suppose it was the best thing to do."

"So, aside from all that, what did you learn about the map?" Tom asked.

"Well, each piece was definitely buried in a different part of the world," Jessie replied, "just like that book of yours said."

"And where are the others now?"

"They used to belong to three separate people," Henry answered. "But according to those pages we copied, they're now all owned by some millionaire named Winston Walker. He's the man who found the last piece before Benny found his. He bought the first two and found the third."

"Did you find pictures of the other three?" Grandfather asked.

"No, just one," Jessie said. "Violet drew a copy of it and then joined it to Benny's. There's a number '1' at the bottom of it, so it looks as though we've got pieces number one and four."

"If we could put all the pieces together," Violet continued, "they would make a perfect square. The piece Benny found belongs in the bottom right-hand corner, and the piece I drew from the book goes in the top left."

"Once you find pictures of the other two," Tom said, "you'll be the first people to see the complete map in hundreds of years."

"And then we can find the treasure!" Benny said gleefully.

"That's very possible," Tom told him. "Very possible indeed. So what's the next step in your investigation?"

Henry said, "We're thinking of going to the historical society, if there is one around here. Maybe someone there could help us."

"We have one," Tom said. "It's inside the lighthouse on the other side of town, near the miniature golf course. It's like a little museum inside, and there's a library. Plenty of books to go through."

"Sounds like just the right place," Henry said. "I guess we'll head over there first thing in the morning."

"Welcome to Cherrystone Harbor's lighthouse and historical society," the man behind the front desk said the next morning.

He closed the book he was reading and smiled at the Aldens. "My name is Cliff. What brings you kids here today?"

"We were hoping to visit the library," Henry replied.

Cliff patted the book. "Interested in brushing up on your local history?"

"Sort of," Henry said. "We're visiting only for a few days, but we really like the town."

"Oh, I see," Cliff said, nodding. "Well, the library is upstairs and to the left." He pointed to a staircase on the other side of the room.

The children turned to go. "Thank you," Henry told him with a polite wave of his hand.

Fifteen minutes and a lot of huffing and puffing later, the Aldens reached the last step. The library was at the very top of the lighthouse!

It was a simple square room with bookshelves for walls. There was a table in the

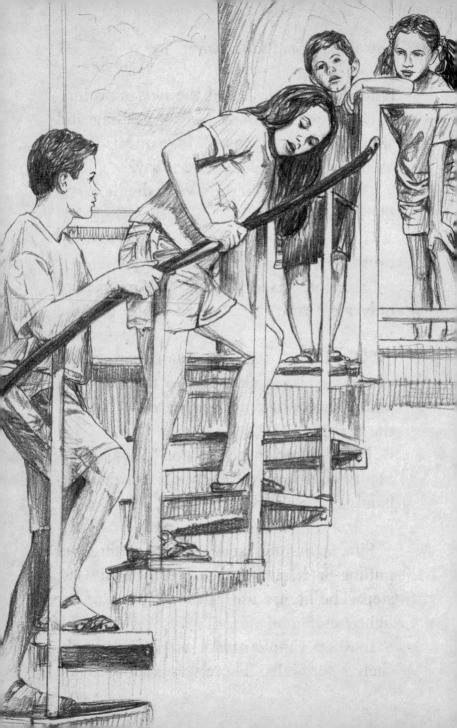

center with a few chairs around it. A window on the left side had been opened, and a cool breeze was blowing the drapes around.

"I'm too tired to even read!" Benny cried, pulling out one of the chairs and slumping into it.

"Yeah, that was quite a climb," Henry commented, wiping the perspiration from his forehead.

Could John Finney's treasure be worth all this?

"Well, I guess we should get busy," Henry suggested, and with that the Aldens began their hunt for information.

This time they decided to keep an eye out for *any* book that sounded as though it might tell them something about John Finney or his treasure.

Nearly an hour later, after it seemed as though they had gone through every book in the room, Jessie said, "I vote we spend the afternoon at the beach and forget about John Finney's treasure for the rest of the day!"

"Me, too!" Benny cried out.

"Great idea," Violet said wearily as she closed another volume.

"Yeah, I guess we should take a break," Henry agreed, looking out the window at the beautiful blue sky.

"We're not going to have any luck here," Jessie said, taking a seat next to Violet. "I've looked through all the books on my side of the room, and so has Benny. And Violet has only two left."

Henry frowned. "Okay, perhaps we'll go someplace else tomorrow. Any idea where else we might — "

"Oh, my goodness, look at this!" Violet yelped. She held open the second-to-last book. On the right-hand page was a picture of one of the map pieces.

And it wasn't one of the two the Aldens already had.

"What's it say, Violet? Read it! And then we've got to draw a copy of that piece!"

Violet set the book flat in front of her. "Okay. According to the text, the piece shown here is piece number two. It was found accidentally by a man digging a well in Italy in 1872. It was passed down through his family until eight years ago, when Winston Walker bought it for eleven thousand dollars."

"Wow!" Henry exclaimed.

"There's some more information about the first piece," Violet went on, "but nothing we don't know." She smiled as she read on. "It also says that the fourth and final piece has yet to be found." She looked up at Benny. "You took care of that, didn't you?"

"Sure did!" Benny said.

Violet read some more, and as she did, her smile disappeared as quickly as it had come.

"What's wrong?" Jessie asked.

Violet slid the book across to her sister, pointing to a paragraph. Henry and Benny came around and read along over her shoulder. The more they all read, the deeper their hearts sank.

"Oh, no . . ." Jessie said in a whisper.

" 'Oh, no' is right," Henry agreed. "Let's

get out of here. After we get back from the beach, we've got some serious thinking to do."

As planned, the children spent the rest of the day along the shore, enjoying the sunshine. In the meantime, Grandfather helped Tom do some repairs on the top floor of the house.

Violet collected a few more shells, then sat on her blanket in the sand and put two necklaces together. She gave one to Jessie, who was lying next to her. Henry and Benny spent most of the time in the water. There were a few people reading the newspaper from the day before, and that worried the Aldens a bit. But happily no one made the connection between the boy whose picture was on the front page and the one who was swimming around in the ocean.

The Aldens left the beach at around four o'clock to head back to Tom's. They looked like typical tourists with their sandals and their towels slung over their shoulders.

Just before they reached Tom's street, a shiny black limousine pulled up to the curb next to them. The back window came down, and a man dressed in a suit leaned forward.

"Excuse me," he said with a smile. "Would you happen to be the Alden children?"

Henry said, "Er . . . yes." The man was smiling, but for some reason Henry didn't think he could be trusted.

The man looked down at Benny. "Then you must be the little boy who found the bottle the other day."

"Y-yes, that's right," Benny said.

The man put out his hand to shake. A diamond ring on his fourth finger sparkled in the afternoon sunlight. "Pleased to meet you."

"Uh, you, too," Benny replied. He didn't want to shake the man's hand, but he didn't want to be rude, either.

The man reached into the pocket of his suit jacket and took out an envelope. Then he held it open so the children could see what was inside — a thick wad of fresh twenty-dollar bills.

"There's a thousand dollars in here. That's a lot of money for a little boy like you. You can have it if I can have that bottle you found. In fact, I don't even want the bottle. I'd just like to have what's inside it."

"Uh, I don't think so," Benny said.

"Really? May I ask why?" said the man.

"Because I'd have to talk to my grandfather first," Benny told him.

"Yes," Jessie said, coming forward and putting her arms around her little brother. "We would have to talk to our grandfather."

The man pretended to look hurt. "Oh, do we have to get him involved? Can't we just make a deal right here?"

"I'm sorry," Henry cut in, "but we really shouldn't be talking to strangers in the first place."

The man's smile suddenly came back. "That's very smart," he said, although he didn't sound as if he meant it.

Then he reached into his pocket again

and took out a business card. "Well, when you're ready to make a deal, after you've talked to your grandfather, please give me a call."

"Ummm, okay," Henry said, looking over the card quickly.

"Have a nice day, children," the man told them as the window went back up. Then the car pulled away and was gone.

The others huddled around Henry to see what was on the card. There was nothing but a name and a phone number, and the name made their hearts jump:

Winston Walker
1-732-555-0241

"I think we'd better get back and tell Grandfather and Tom about this," Henry said sullenly.

"I think you're right," Jessie replied. "Let's go."

CHAPTER 5

An Unwelcome Visitor

"I'm not surprised Walker turned up," Tom said as he brought his fork to his mouth. He and Grandfather had made reservations at a nice restaurant called the Crab's Claw Inn, right on Oyster Bay. "He has obviously been after John Finney's treasure for years."

"But how did he get here so fast?" Violet wondered aloud. "Does he live around here?"

"No," Tom said, "but a man with that much money travels all the time." Tom snapped his fingers. "He can be anywhere in an instant. He probably saw the story in the paper."

"Speaking of which," Grandfather said, reaching into his jacket pocket, "look at this." He opened the front page of a different newspaper. This one was called the *Daily Tribune*, and there was Benny's face again. It was the same picture as last time.

"This is one of the biggest newspapers on the East Coast," Grandfather said. "Your story is getting around fast. Pretty soon Winston Walker will have a lot of competition for that treasure."

"So what do we do?" asked Jessie.

"You don't have to do anything if you don't want to," Tom replied. "Or you can take Winston Walker's offer if you wish." He looked at Benny. "It's your piece of the map, Benny, so it's your decision."

Benny had been playing with his food but not eating it. The others were beginning to get worried. It was a rare moment when Benny wasn't hungry.

"I want to keep it," he said firmly.

"So then keep it," Tom told him. "Have you found out anything about the other pieces?"

The children looked at one another with silent, somber faces, which puzzled Tom. "What's wrong?"

"We got a picture of one of them, piece number two, but the third piece, well . . . that's the one Winston Walker found, and . . . he'll never let anyone else see it or photograph it. He's the only one who knows what it looks like. That's what the book in the Lighthouse Library said."

Tom looked at Grandfather, then back at Henry. "So what are you going to do?"

"We're not sure yet," Henry admitted. "We were thinking maybe we could put the other three pieces together and figure out where the treasure is from there, but . . ."

Tom frowned. "I doubt John Finney would make it that easy. Knowing him, he probably made sure you needed all four pieces."

"That's what we figured, too," Jessie said.

Henry sighed, then smiled. "We'll think of something," he told them. He wanted to keep a positive outlook on the situation. But deep down inside, neither he nor any of the other Alden children had a clue as to what that something would be.

After they all got back from the restaurant, Tom and Grandfather turned in for the night. The children, on the other hand, decided to play a card game. They sat on one of the beds in the boys' room. Watch was lying on the carpet near the doorway. Playing games with one another was something the Aldens always enjoyed. But tonight they enjoyed it even more because it helped them forget all about John Finney's treasure for a little while.

"Do you have a . . . seven?" Jessie asked Benny, holding all her cards in a fan.

Benny giggled. "Nope! Go fish!"

Jessie frowned and took another card from the deck. Then she groaned and took another. By the time she got to her fifth,

she was rolling her eyes and groaning. "Who taught him how to be such a good card-player?"

"Grandfather," Henry said. "Remember? He taught all of us how to play."

Caught up in their card game, the Aldens didn't hear what was happening in Tom's backyard. But Watch did hear something. He got up and hurried out of the room. The children, still playing cards, didn't notice him.

When Watch got to the first floor, he ran to the door that led to Tom's study and sniffed along the bottom. Then he began growling loudly.

"Do you hear that?" Violet asked. "I think it's Watch." The children ran out of the room and hurried down the stairs.

"Watch, be quiet!" Henry said when he got to the bottom. But Watch just kept barking and scratching at the door.

"He must hear something in there!" Violet said.

Without hesitating, Henry opened the door and pushed it back. Then he reached over and flicked on the light. The intruder was almost all the way out the window. If the children had waited another second or so, they wouldn't have seen anyone at all.

Watch zoomed across the carpet, but the thief jumped down just in time. Then he — or she — hurried across the lawn, swiftly scaled the fence, and disappeared into the night.

Henry snapped his fingers. "Just missed 'em!"

Grandfather and Tom appeared in the doorway. "What's all this racket?" Grandfather asked.

"There was someone in here!" Benny replied. He looked scared, so Violet came up behind him and draped her arms around him.

"What?" Tom said. "Did you see the person's face?"

Henry shook his head. "No. When I turned on the light, the person was almost out the window."

"How strange," Tom said. "Nothing like that has ever happened here. Someone must know we have the fourth piece of the map."

He went outside and apologized to the other guests who had awoken because of the noise. If any of them wanted to go to another bed-and-breakfast, he told them, he'd understand. But they all said no, they wanted to stay. They knew it wasn't Tom's fault. Since everything seemed to be under control, they all went back to bed.

Coming back into his study, Tom said, "Is anything missing?"

"Here's the bottle," Jessie said, standing by the desk.

"And there's the piece of the map," Henry said, pointing to it on the table.

"But why didn't the person take it?" Jessie asked.

"That's what I'd like to know," Tom said quietly. "Even if he wanted to draw a copy of it, he couldn't do it in the dark. Is it possible he just put it down and forgot about it?"

"Maybe he — " Henry began, but then someone came walking into the room.

It was an elderly woman in slippers and

a robe. Her hair was the off-white color of old piano keys, and it ran down her back in a long ponytail. She held the robe tightly around her body, as if she were chilly. "Tom? What happened?"

"Oh, hello, Mrs. Carter. How are you?" Tom asked.

"I'm fine, but you don't look so good. I heard all the commotion," Mrs. Carter said.

"We had a break-in," Tom told her. "Mrs. Carter, these are some friends of mine. This is James Alden, and these are his grandchildren, Henry, Jessie, Violet, and the little fellow is Benny. Kids, this is Mary Carter. She's my next-door neighbor."

Mrs. Carter and the Aldens exchanged hellos. Then the woman said, "A break-in? Was anything taken?"

"It doesn't appear so."

"What were those flashes?"

Everyone looked confused.

"Flashes?" Jessie asked.

Mrs. Carter pointed to the windows. "There were flashes in here. I saw them from my sitting room while I was watching

TV. Quick bursts of light. About a dozen."

Tom said, "I'm afraid I don't —"

"Pictures!" Violet blurted out. "Someone was taking pictures! The light bursts were caused by the flash!"

Tom sighed and nodded. "Yeah, that's probably exactly what it was. There are so many reporters and other treasure hunters around here now, it could've been anybody. John Finney's treasure is probably so valuable, some people will risk getting arrested for breaking into someone's house in order to get their hands on it."

Then Grandfather added, "So, as you said, it could've been anybody."

"Uh-huh, that's right. But no matter who it was," Tom replied, "they've got pictures of the last piece of the map now. So if you kids really want to find that treasure, I suggest you do it as soon as possible."

CHAPTER 6

Danger, Danger, Everywhere!

The next morning the children and their grandfather went to a little shopping village that they had spotted when they first got into town. Originally the children had planned to go alone, but now Grandfather insisted on going with them. Soon after they arrived, however, they split up because the children wanted to get their grandfather a souvenir.

There were dozens of tiny stores in the village, each with its own specialty. One sold nothing but kites, another sold saltwater taffy, and another sold beach items such as bathing suits, suntan oil, and folding chairs. The first store they went into was called Treasures in the Sand.

Jessie saw the sign. "Haven't we had enough trouble with stuff we've found in the sand?" she said with a groan. The others laughed.

Once inside, each Alden went to a different part of the store. Violet was drawn to a rack of matted photos, sketches, and paintings. The ones that she liked she set aside for the others to see.

She had just found a beautiful watercolor of an ocean sunset when she noticed the two men outside. They were standing on the sidewalk, with people moving all around them. One had a little notebook, and a copy of yesterday's newspaper was sticking out of his back pocket. He also had a pencil tucked behind one ear. The second man had a camera hanging around his neck. Both were watching Benny through the window with great interest. It didn't take Violet long to figure out who they were — a reporter/photographer team.

Benny was looking for a price sticker on a seagull sculpture when the reporter pointed at him. Then the man said something to the photographer, who brought his camera up to take a shot.

"Benny!" Violet said sharply.

Startled, Benny almost dropped the sculpture.

"Yes?"

"Come here for a second. You've got to see this!" Violet said.

Benny walked away just in time. Both the photographer and the reporter looked disappointed. Then they moved closer to the window, determined to find out where Benny had gone.

"What?" Benny asked. "What do you want to show me?"

Violet didn't have an answer ready. "Huh? Oh . . . this, isn't this nice?" she asked clumsily, showing him the sunset painting.

"Uh, yeah, I guess so."

"There's an even nicer one over there," Violet said after the two men found Benny again. She took him by the arm and quickly led him to the other side of the store. Then she looked back briefly and saw the men hurrying around to the other window. They had figured out what she was up to.

She went to Henry and Jessie, who were standing together, talking quietly.

"I think we've got a problem," said Violet.

"What? What's wrong?" asked Jessie.

Violet said, "I'm not going to turn around, but there are two men outside. One has a notebook and the other has a camera. They're trying to get a picture of Benny."

Trying to appear as casual as possible, Henry and Jessie glanced over Violet's shoulder and saw the two men.

"Reporters," Jessie said with a sigh.

"I'm sure," Violet said.

"Wh-what are we going to do?" Benny asked.

"I've got an idea," Jessie said. "Stay here.

I'll be right back. Benny, come and stand behind Henry and Violet so those two men can't get any pictures of you."

Benny eased out of sight, and Jessie went over to the sales counter, where an older woman was reading a magazine with her glasses perched at the end of her nose.

"Excuse me, ma'am?" Jessie said.

The woman looked down at the pretty young girl and pulled off the glasses. They rested against her chest on a beaded chain. "Yes? Can I help you, young lady?"

"Um, well, would you happen to have a back door?" asked Jessie.

"A back door? Yes, through the stockroom, but it's not for customer use," the woman answered.

Jessie looked worried. "Well, could we please use it anyway, my sister and brothers and I?"

"May I ask why?"

Jessie hesitated, unsure of how to answer. Then she sighed. "Because there are two men outside who . . . we'd rather not see."

The woman eyed Jessie suspiciously. "Are you in some kind of trouble?"

"No, no, ma'am, but . . ." Jessie started to say.

The woman turned toward the window. The reporter and photographer didn't notice. They were too busy waiting for Benny to make another appearance.

"Why does that man have a camera?" the woman demanded.

"I think he's a photographer for a newspaper," Jessie said. "Please, we really need to —"

Suddenly a smile spread across the woman's face. "Are you the children who found that bottle, the one with the map in it?"

"Yes, ma'am," Jessie said.

"Did you find the pirate's treasure?" the woman asked.

"Miss," Jessie said firmly, "we really need to get out of here. Can we use the back door, please?"

The woman's smile disappeared. "Well, okay, I guess in this case it'll be all right."

"Thank you," Jessie replied.

The woman led the Aldens to a small door located in a quiet corner at the back of the store.

"Thank you very much, ma'am," Henry told the lady as he and the others went out. The bright afternoon sun came flooding in around them.

"If you find that treasure, don't forget about me," she said. The children only smiled.

Now they were standing in the alleyway between Treasures in the Sand and the surf shop next door. At one end they could see people on the busy sidewalk. The other led to a large parking lot.

"It's not going to take those two long to figure out what happened," Henry said.

"I think we should go back to the parking lot," Violet offered.

"Good idea," Henry agreed.

It seemed for a moment that they would get away cleanly. But no sooner had they reached the end of the alley than someone at the other end shouted, "There they are!"

All the children turned at the same time. The reporter and photographer were standing there. Everyone remained still for just a second, then the two men started running.

"Let's go!" Henry cried, and the Aldens took off.

The children reached the other end of the lot at the same time the two men exited the alleyway.

"We need to go back!" Jessie said breathlessly.

"Back? You mean the way we came?" Henry asked, still running.

"No, back to the sidewalk, where all the people are!" Jessie told him. "We'll lose them in the crowd."

As if they had rehearsed it a hundred times, all four children turned right at exactly the same moment. They ran up a gently sloping driveway that led to the main road, then made a sharp left turn when they got to the sidewalk.

As Jessie had predicted, there were people everywhere. And since the Aldens were smaller than most of them, they had little trouble blending into the crowd and becoming invisible to the newspapermen.

"Now what do we do?" Violet asked. "They'll keep looking until they find us!"

"Do you see Grandfather anywhere?" Jessie asked.

Henry took a long and careful look around. "No, nowhere."

"Let's go into one of the stores!" Benny suggested.

Jessie ran a hand through her little brother's hair. "That's our Benny, always thinking."

"We can hide in that saltwater taffy place!" he added.

"Yeah, that's our Benny," Henry said. "Always thinking . . . about food!"

The children laughed. "It's a good idea, Benny," Jessie said, "but we really should hide in a store that no one would expect us to go in."

"Well, we'd better hurry," Violet pointed out. "Those two men should be coming up that driveway any moment!"

The children looked around for just the

right shop. Which one looked the least interesting to a youngster?

"There!" Jessie said, pointing. "The antique place!"

The others turned and saw the sign YESTERYEAR ANTIQUES.

"Hey!" Violet protested. "I like antiques!"

Jessie grabbed her sister's hand and took off. Henry and Benny followed close behind. "I know. I do, too. But who would think to look for four children there?" Jessie said.

Henry looked back to see if the two men had made it to the street yet. They appeared just as the children reached the front door of the shop. Fortunately the men didn't notice.

A little silver bell jingled as the children went in. "Let's get to the back, where they won't be able to see us if they walk by," Henry said.

The back of the store was dimly lit and smelled of must and mildew — as if the whole building were as much of an antique

as the things that were in it. The Aldens
found themselves surrounded by hundreds
of fascinating items from years past: dishes,
furniture, paintings, and even some old
toys. It didn't take them long to forget
about the two men who had been chasing
them. There was so much to see!

For the first time in the last fifteen minutes, they felt as though they could relax.
There was nothing to fear here, in the quiet
back room of this peaceful little store.

Or was there?

"Well, hello there," a deep and familiar
voice said. The children froze. Then they
turned and saw someone standing in the
open doorway.

Winston Walker.

"Oh, no," Jessie said softly.

Walker looked positively delighted. He
clapped his hands once, then rubbed them
together. "What a pleasant surprise! I
didn't know you children were lovers of fine
antiques!"

"We're not," Henry told him. "We're just
looking for a present. For our grandfather."

Walker's face lit up with joy. "A present? How very thoughtful of all of you! What do you have in mind?"

"We haven't decided yet," Jessie said. She didn't like the way Walker was talking to them. The words were nice, but the way he said them made it sound like he didn't mean them.

"Well, there are lots of nice things in here. I come here all the time. It's one of my favorite stores down on the shore. Of course, most of the things in here are very expensive. Possibly more expensive than you children could afford."

None of the Aldens liked the sound of this. How did he know what they could and couldn't afford?

"However, if you kids had a little more money in your pockets, then I'm sure you could have anything in here that you wanted."

"Maybe," Henry said with a frown. Now he wasn't sure what was worse — being outside with those two men or being in here with the snobby Winston Walker.

Walker stroked his chin thoughtfully. "Now, let's see, how could you kids get some more money? Hmmm." He snapped his fingers and looked brightly at Benny. "I know! You, young man, could sell me that piece of the map that you found! And this time, I'll double my first offer to *two* thousand dollars. Now, that's a lot of money for a little fellow like you to have. I never had two thousand dollars when I was your age — whatever that age might be. So, do we have a deal, young man?" Walker said, taking his wallet out of his back pocket. "It just so happens that I have the cash on me right now."

"Even if he said yes, he doesn't have the piece of the map with him," Jessie said.

This didn't seem to bother Winston Walker at all. "That's quite all right, quite all right. I'll come by the house in which you're staying and pick it up later. I trust you."

"How do you know where we're staying?" Violet asked suspiciously. The others were wondering the same thing.

"Oh, I make it my business to know such things. Yes indeed." Walker carefully counted out twenty hundred-dollar bills, then held them out to Benny. "So, my young friend, do we have a deal or don't we?"

"I really shouldn't without my grand —" Benny began to say.

Mr. Walker's charm slipped away for a second. "Him again!" he barked. The children froze.

Then Walker's smile returned. "I mean . . . him? Well, maybe I could throw in a little extra just to be nice."

"Grandfather's not interested in your money!" Jessie said.

"Oh, is that right? Well, good for him. I admire that." He looked back at the youngest Alden. "So what do you say, Billy?"

"It's Benny," Benny corrected him.

"Huh? Oh, yes, of course. So how about it, Benny? Would you sell me that piece of the map?" Winston Walker asked.

"I'm sorry," Jessie said, taking Benny by

the hand and leading him back toward the front of the store, "but we have to be going now. We've got to find our grandfather."

"But I — I . . ." The Aldens didn't hear the rest of Winston Walker's sentence. Newspaper reporters or not, they would rather be running around in the crowd than in a little antique store with that rude man.

Fortunately, neither the reporter nor the photographer were anywhere in sight. The children found their grandfather about fifteen minutes later, looking for something to read in a paperback bookstore.

CHAPTER 7

The Helpful Mr. Ford

After hearing of his grandchildren's latest adventure, James Alden decided they would eat dinner that night in the kitchen rather than on the front porch, where they might be seen.

As they all quietly ate their meals, Tom read the latest article about John Finney's treasure in a paper called the *Atlantic Informer*. The picture of Benny that Meredith Baker had taken on the beach was still the only one the newspapers had, so they kept running it over and over again.

"Says here John Finney's treasure is probably worth more than ten million dollars," he announced. He stroked his chin and added, "I wonder who made up that number?"

Violet, who was looking down at another paper while cutting her steak, said, "This one says it's worth only four million."

"Mine says six," Benny chimed in through a mouthful of mashed potatoes.

"Mine says six, too," Jessie added. Her newspaper was the same one that ran the first story and picture a few days before.

Tom said, "Maybe it *is* six."

Henry shook his head. "I don't know. This one here says twelve."

Tom whistled. "Wow, twelve million dollars. That's quite a high price to put on a treasure no one's even seen in nearly two hundred years."

All the wild stories surrounding the map and the treasure had become so silly that neither Tom nor the Aldens could take them seriously anymore.

"Hey, Benny, according to this story,

you're eleven," Violet said, giggling. "I didn't know you were older than me!"

Grandfather said in a grumpy voice, "And the *Atlantic Informer* thinks you're from California."

"The next one will say I'm from Mars!" Benny told them, and everyone, including Grandfather, broke out into laughter.

When things settled down, Grandfather said, "We really will have to do something soon, before the situation gets any worse."

"Like what?" Henry asked.

"Like either you try to find the treasure or you let Winston Walker have the last piece of the map," suggested Grandfather.

"I . . . I don't like that second idea," Benny said.

"I don't, either," said Jessie. Violet and Henry nodded in agreement.

"Then you've got to find the treasure without that missing piece," said Grandfather. "And that's not going to be very e —"

The front doorbell rang. Tom got up to answer it. He knew it couldn't be one of the guests because they all had keys.

The man Tom found on his front porch was so tall and muscular that he almost looked like a giant. A tiny blue knapsack was slung over his shoulder.

"Can I help you?" Tom asked.

"Is this the house where the boy who found the old bottle is staying?" the man asked.

"Can I ask what your interest in the boy is?" Tom wanted to know.

"My name's Jack Ford. I used to work for Winston Walker," said the man. "I was with him in Brazil when he found the third piece of the map. I have a feeling you'd like to know what it looks like."

Tom just stood there, speechless. Then he invited Jack Ford inside.

They all went into Tom's study. Jack sat in the comfortable chair by the fireplace, his knapsack lying beside him like a sleeping dog.

"First of all, you should know that Winston Walker is a bit crazy. He's obsessed with that treasure," Jack began.

"Obsessed?" Benny repeated, not sure what the word meant.

"He thinks about it all the time," Jack said, pointing to his own head. "It's like the only thing in the world that he cares about."

"Oh . . . yeah," Benny said. "We already noticed *that*."

"Why were you in Brazil with him?" Henry asked.

"I was a digger, which means I was good with a shovel," said Jack. "I'd been all around the world doing that kind of work. But working for Winston Walker was a horrible job. He made us sleep in ratty tents and eat lousy food. We had to work nonstop ten hours a day, and we didn't get Saturdays and Sundays off."

Violet said, "That's terrible."

"That's exactly what he was," said Jack, nodding.

"Then why did you keep working for him?" Jessie asked.

Jack frowned. "Because I thought there'd be a big payoff. I thought as soon as the job was finished, he was going to give us all a huge chunk of money."

"Why did you think that?"

"He told us whoever found the next piece of the map would get a huge bonus."

Benny said, "*You* found it, didn't you?"

"Yes, I did. It was under a big banana tree, about a foot down in the ground."

"In a bottle?" Benny guessed.

"Uh-huh, the exact same type of bottle you found," Jack told him. "I was by myself, and I ground out the cork with a stick. I wanted to make sure the piece of paper inside was part of John Finney's treasure map before I went yelling about it. About a year earlier, some other guy thought he'd found it, but he was wrong. Winston Walker fired him."

"How mean," Jessie said.

"Winston Walker could be very mean when he was angry. Like I said, he wasn't the nicest guy in the world. But anyway, I shook the paper out of the bottle, and sure enough, it was the third piece of the map," Jack said.

"What did Walker do?" Henry asked.

"Well, I went over and showed it to him,

and he was as excited as a little kid. All the other workers cheered and carried me around on their shoulders. That night, Walker took us to a nice restaurant. The next morning he gave us our money and sent us back to the United States. But I never got that bonus he promised. He said he'd send it to me, but he never did. In fact, I never heard from him again."

Grandfather said, "Was it a lot of money, if you don't mind my asking?"

"It was five thousand dollars. That might not be a lot of money to him, but it sure was a lot to me. Still is." Jack went on to tell them that he had been sending money to his mother back in the United States. She lived alone and didn't have enough money. He had told her about the bonus, then called her when he found the piece of the map. They were both very excited. He promised to give her the money so she could finish paying for her house.

"That's so awful," Violet said sadly. "And to think I felt sorry for Winston Walker."

"Oh, you still should," Jack replied. "His

greed is a disease, just as bad as any other, and worse than some. It controls him."

"So then why have you come here?" Tom asked. "I mean, why are you so willing to tell us what the third piece looks like? How come you're not interested in getting the piece Benny found so you can have the treasure for yourself?"

"Because I don't want to end up like Walker," Jack replied. He became thoughtful. "If I found the treasure and became rich, I might start acting like him and thinking like him. He thinks money brings you happiness, but he's one of the unhappiest people I've ever known. And because he's so unhappy, he makes other people unhappy. I'm not saying *all* rich people are unhappy, but he certainly is."

Suddenly Violet *did* feel sorry for Walker all over again, although she didn't say so.

"I made a promise to myself — if I was alive when the last piece was found, I swore I would go to the people who found it and let them know what the third one looked like. I know Winston Walker hasn't let anyone else see it. Only two people in the world know what it looks like — Winston and I." Jack took a sip of the lemonade Tom had given him. "Either way, I've always had a good memory, and I know exactly what's on that third piece. I'll be glad to tell you about it. I saw Benny's picture in the paper while I was at my home in upstate New York. I'm glad that someone else has a chance to find that treasure."

Tom took out the drawing that Violet had made of the three pieces of the map and laid it on the table. The missing part was in the lower left-hand corner.

With pencil in hand, Jack slowly and carefully began adding the final images. There were some more trees, a few rocks, and, strangely, a bird sitting on its nest. He drew six of these, all of equal size.

"Is that a . . . a nesting bird?" Jessie asked.

"Yes. I was surprised by that, too. I'm not sure what it means. Birds nest all over the world," said Jack.

"This is probably the first time anyone's

seen this map in its complete form in two hundred years," Tom said almost in a whisper.

"Can you tell where the treasure is, Mr. Harrison?" asked Henry.

Tom scratched his head. "No, not yet. I guess it would be safe to say this is the ocean over here," he said, pointing to the squiggly lines. "And these trees . . . well, they could be any trees. Same with the rocks. But the birds . . . why do they seem familiar?"

He walked around the room, stroking his chin while the others kept studying the map. He stopped at the window and stared into the backyard. There were some birds fluttering around the feeder he had hung from one of the trees. He watched them for a moment, hoping they would help him remember. But nothing happened.

And then it hit him.

"The nature trail!"

Everyone turned at once. "Huh?" Henry grunted.

"There's a nature trail over near the bicycle path. I used to go there with my students. About a mile down, there's a bird sanctuary. The Department of Environmental Protection declared the area a protected nesting site so no one could build on it. Birds have been nesting there for hundreds of years!" Tom rushed over and looked at the completed map again. "That has to be it. It has to be. And this part here, where the X is . . ." He tapped the spot with his fingers. "That must be the little grove of pine trees. They're very, very old. That has to be it," he said again, softly to himself. "It *has* to be. . . ."

CHAPTER 8

The Final Offer

"Okay, so do we have it all figured out?" Tom asked, rubbing his eyes and yawning. It was nearly ten o'clock now.

Jack Ford had been gone for about two hours. Before he left, he wished them all good luck. He had shown no interest in finding the treasure.

Henry nodded. "I think so. We all get up before sunrise. You and I go to the shed in the backyard and get the shovels. Then we load them into Grandfather's station wagon, which is parked around the corner."

"Right," Tom said.

"While we're doing that, everyone else can gather up some food and something to drink," Henry said. "And then we all sneak out to the car and head for the nature trail."

"Now, what happens if we don't —" Jessie began, then was abruptly cut off.

"Well, isn't this nice?" said a deep, powerful voice. All heads jerked up, and there in the doorway stood Winston Walker.

"How did you —" Tom began.

"The front door was open, so I let myself in," Walker replied.

"What do you want?" asked Grandfather.

Walker folded his arms and smiled. "I think you all know why I'm here. You have something that I want."

"The last piece of the map," Henry said.

"Exactly right. I'm guessing the reason you didn't take my latest offer was because it was too low. I should've known. Two thousand dollars doesn't buy much these days. So, I'm prepared to make it three thousand."

Walker let his offer linger for a moment.

"No? Then how about four? I'm afraid that's my final offer."

"What do you think, Benny?" Grandfather asked. "You found the bottle, so it's your decision. Whatever you want to do is fine with us. Right, kids?" They all agreed that it was.

"I'm sorry, Mr. Walker, but I don't think I'd like to do that," said Benny. After all that had happened, he wanted to find the treasure for himself.

Walker began tapping his right foot, and his hands went into his pockets. Suddenly his smile seemed forced. "May I ask why, Benny?"

"I . . . I just don't want to," Benny answered.

"I'm sorry, Mr. Walker," Tom said, "but since Benny obviously isn't interested in making a deal with you, I'm afraid I'll have to ask you to —"

"I don't understand!" Winston Walker said forcefully, his face turning red. "I'm offering you four thousand dollars! In *cash*!

No kid has that kind of money! All you have to do is give me that lousy little piece of paper that you found on the beach!"

"But he doesn't want to," Jessie said angrily.

"Mr. Walker —" Tom started saying, but the millionaire didn't seem to hear him.

"I've been looking for that treasure longer than anyone! I have a right to it! I've spent thousands of dollars and half my life trying to find it! It belongs to me! ME!"

No one said anything. They just stared. Walker looked as though he were about to explode.

Then Grandfather stood up, walked to Tom's desk, opened the top drawer, and took out the piece of the map that Benny had found. Winston Walker's entire manner changed instantly. His eyes widened and his smile returned.

"Is that it?" he asked excitedly.

"Yes, it is," Grandfather answered. "This is the fourth and final piece to Captain John Finney's treasure map."

"Can . . . can I have it?" Walker asked, reaching toward it from the other side of the room.

Grandfather shook his head. "No, you can't. My grandson found it, which means it belongs to him, and he already said you can't have it."

"Now, look here," Walker began sternly, taking a quick step toward Grandfather Alden.

Grandfather grabbed the telephone off its cradle and held it up. "Mr. Walker, my good friend Tom, who I might remind you is the owner of this house, has already asked you once to leave. I'm now asking you a second time. If you don't do so at once, I will have no choice but to call the local police. They are as aware of all this treasure business as you are, and I'm sure they wouldn't appreciate a wealthy and important gentleman like yourself giving a group of innocent youngsters a hard time." Grandfather's face was serious.

A heavy silence hung in the room. All eyes shifted to Winston Walker, but no one moved. Walker seemed to be thinking over Grandfather's statement.

Walker's expression was transformed from one of helplessness back to thinly contained rage. "All right, Mr. Alden. You win. I can see I'm not going to get anywhere with you people."

"Maybe if you had been a little kinder, things would be different," Grandfather Alden told him.

For just a brief moment, Walker seemed confused again, as if the idea of being kind were the most bizarre thing in the world. Then he smiled and said, "It doesn't really matter what might have been, Mr. Alden, because I'll find another way. I didn't become such a wealthy and successful man by giving up a fight this easily." He stormed across the room toward the door. "This isn't over yet, not by a long shot!" he growled. He seemed to be talking to himself. "You'll hear from me again!" he called out just before he slammed the front door shut. And then he was gone.

"We're going to have to keep our eyes

and ears open," Tom said. "One thing he said was absolutely true — he's not the kind of man who gives up easily. I have a feeling we'll hear from him again."

"Probably," Grandfather said.

"So what do we do now?" Henry asked.

Grandfather replied, "We stick to our plan for tomorrow."

"Really?" Benny said with great enthusiasm.

"Really. Winston Walker's not the only one who doesn't give up, right?"

"Right!" Benny cheered.

"Okay, then, let's go over the plan one more time," Grandfather told them.

CHAPTER 9

What You See Is What You Get

"We're almost there," Tom said, huffing and puffing. It was a very hot day.

"I hope I have enough strength left to dig!" Benny said.

"You will," Henry told him. "If no one digs, we won't find the treasure."

The Aldens' plan to escape early in the morning so none of the newspaper people would see them had worked perfectly. There hadn't been a single reporter or photographer in sight.

"I wish I'd brought my camera," Violet said as she walked down the sunlit trail. The tall reeds on either side of the path created a sort of natural corridor, hiding the group from plain view. "This is such a pretty place."

The path brought them to a small footbridge that spanned a shallow stream, then curved sharply to the left before leading them into an open field.

"And there are the birds," Tom said.

There were hundreds of them scattered all over the place, sitting on their little nests made of twigs and straw. They looked up curiously at the visitors, but none of them seemed too alarmed.

"Wow," Violet said in a whisper.

"I'll bet John Finney saw the very same thing," Henry said.

"Maybe he stood just where we're standing just now!" Benny guessed.

"That's possible," Tom replied. "And look over there."

He pointed a little farther down the path. There in the distance, standing out from the other trees, was a small crowd of crooked pines.

"The pine trees!" Benny said.

"Yep," Tom told him. "If the treasure's not buried in there somewhere, then I have no idea where it is."

"Are we ready to find out?" Grandfather asked.

"Ready," Henry said, patting his shovel.

Checking the map one more time, Tom made his best guess as to exactly where the treasure was buried. Then he and Grandfather sat back and let the children do the digging. The loose, sandy soil was easy to cut into, but the growing heat of the day made the work exhausting.

After about an hour the children had made a hole nearly four feet deep and just as wide. Then they stopped to take a rest and have a drink.

"Boy, I'm beat!" Henry said as he poured out a cup of the ice-cold lemonade for Jessie. "And that hole's pretty deep. How far down could the treasure be?"

"Maybe we're not digging in the right place," Violet pointed out.

Tom studied the map again. "Well, if it's not here, then I know one or two other places it might be, but that's about it. I still think it's here, though."

"What if we don't find it?" Benny wondered.

"Then we don't find it," Jessie answered. "We'll be no worse off than we are now."

Benny considered this for a moment, then nodded. "That's true."

Grandfather smiled. He was proud of his grandchildren for not being so concerned with finding the treasure. They were happy on the inside, and finding or not finding the treasure wouldn't change that.

Henry took another long sip from his cup, then set it aside and said, "Well, I'm going to get back to work. If the treasure's down there, we've got to find it."

Then a voice — an unpleasantly familiar one — said, "Yes, you do. You've got to find it so you can give it to *me*."

Once again Winston Walker appeared

out of nowhere. "So nice to see you all again," he said with his usual charm. "And it's even nicer to see that you've started digging already."

"How did you find us?" Jessie asked. She couldn't help it. "You never had the last piece."

"I know, but shortly after I left you all, I was paid a visit by a charming little photographer lady." He pulled a picture out of his pocket and held it up for everyone to see. "And look what she had for me — a very nice shot of the last piece of the map. Seems she was in the right place at the right time a few nights ago."

"Meredith Baker," Jessie said.

"Yes, I believe that was her name," said Winston Walker. "She's quite a businesswoman. This picture cost me a pretty penny, but at least it led me here. I congratulate you youngsters on your detective skills. It seems as though you have solved the mystery of the pirate's map. And I was hoping to do that myself," Walker told them.

"They haven't found the treasure yet, Mr. Walker," Grandfather said sharply.

"I can see that. But if they do, I know they'll be sensible and hand it over to me. After all, I'm the one who's spent half of his life searching for it."

The children looked at one another as they stood in the hole they'd dug. Then Benny sighed and said, "You can have whatever we find, Mr. Walker. It seems like you want it a lot more than we do. We don't need it."

A smile spread across Winston Walker's face. "That's just what I wanted to hear."

Grandfather and Tom both smiled, too, but not for the same reason. They were proud of the children, proud of the way they decided not to fight with Winston Walker over the treasure. They weren't controlled by greed like he was.

So they went back to digging, and Walker watched them with great eagerness. No one spoke, no one laughed, no one even smiled. The fun seemed to have gone out of this treasure hunt for the Aldens. Now all they wanted to do was find the treasure so they could be done with this business. There were still a few days of their vacation left that they could enjoy.

Another half hour passed, and the hole became another foot deeper. But still there was no sign of any treasure.

Henry was just about to suggest that they try a different spot when his shovel hit something hard —

Clink!

Everyone froze. Walker's eyes widened. He took a step forward.

"What was that?"

"I think I hit something," Henry said. "Something made of metal."

"Keep digging, keep digging!" Walker commanded, making wild gestures with his hands.

Jessie, Violet, and Benny climbed out of the hole to give Henry more room. A little more dirt had to be removed before the object's identity became clear — it was an old iron box.

"Faster! Faster!" Walked urged.

Henry didn't like being bossed around by this man, but he quietly kept digging anyway.

Hardly another moment had passed when Winston Walker finally ran out of patience. Much to everyone's shock and surprise, he jumped into the hole next to Henry, dropped to his knees, and began digging around the box with his bare hands. Soon his expensive clothes were covered with dirt, but he didn't seem to care. "So many years of searching . . ." he mumbled to himself, "and now it's mine . . . all mine. . . ."

It took another fifteen minutes before the box was loose enough to move. Walker put his hands on either side of it and pulled mightily. It came free on the third try.

Tom and the Aldens came forward, and Walker got to his knees. The box was fairly large. There was a small padlock at the front, and it was caked with rust.

The millionaire grabbed a large rock and smacked the lock with all his might. Being so old, it broke off on the first shot.

"And now," he said aloud, "at last . . ."

He pushed the lid back and took a good long look at what was waiting for him inside. Then the smile slowly melted from his face.

Nothing was there except a small, rotted leather pouch.

Winston Walker looked as pale as a ghost. He didn't move for a long time. He just stared at the pouch with wide, unbelieving eyes.

Then he picked it up slowly, looked at it some more, and shook its contents into his other hand. There were only two items inside — a single gold coin and a piece of paper about the same size as each of the map pieces.

"What does it say, Mr. Walker?" Violet asked quietly.

Walker read it once in silence, as if he hadn't heard Violet's question. Then he cleared his throat and began out loud:

Whoever you are, I congratulate you on your cleverness. It is my hope that the adventures you have undertaken to find this have caused the blood in your veins to run both hot and cold. I have devoted most of my life to seeking out excitement, and it was one of my last wishes to help someone else do the same.

As for my riches, you have already found them — this single gold coin. It is all that is left of the great fortune I gathered during my many journeys on the high seas. The rest of it has been given away to my relatives and my friends. In my old age, I find I no longer have any use for it.

My best wishes and congratulations again to you, wise adventurer.

Captain John Alexander Finney

Another moment passed in silence. Winston Walker remained still, staring at the note with his mouth open.

Finally, Benny surprised everyone by crouching down and patting Walker on the back. "Sorry, Mr. Walker," he said quietly. Then he stepped back.

Everyone thought Walker was going to explode in anger. But instead, much to their utter amazement, he just let out one small sigh.

"What have I done?" he asked the Aldens. "I've spent my whole life looking for . . . for nothing. There was never any treasure at all, never. All the time and money I've spent, flying all over the world, day and night, thinking about it. And all the people . . ." He looked at the children. "All the people I've hurt. What have I done?"

Violet stepped forward. "You could start making up for it," she suggested. "It's never too late."

Walker said, "How? How can I undo all of this?"

Grandfather said quickly, "You could start by giving Jack Ford the five thousand dollars you owe him."

"Jack Ford?"

"Yes, the man who found the third piece of the map for you. You promised a five-thousand-dollar bonus to whoever found it, and you never paid up," Grandfather said.

Walker appeared to think about this for a moment, then he nodded slowly. "Yes, yes,

I do remember that. I thought he got that money."

"No, Mr. Walker, he never did. And he was going to use it to help his mother finish paying for her house. Because you never gave him the money, he had to keep working to give her a little extra every few weeks. The house still isn't paid for," said Grandfather.

Walker straightened up. "Then it will be," he said firmly, and there was no doubt in anyone's mind that he meant it. Only part of him was sad now. The other part was angry, not at John Finney for not leaving any treasure, but at himself for all the wicked things he'd done while chasing it. "I'll not only pay for his mother's house, I'll buy her a new one, and him, too."

At that moment someone came running around the bend. Everyone turned and was amazed to find Meredith Baker standing there, huffing and puffing, out of breath.

"Did he hurt any of you?" she asked abruptly.

"Huh?" Benny said.

"That Winston Walker character. Did he hurt any of you?"

Grandfather answered for everyone. "Well, no. Who are you?"

"This is the person who broke into Tom's house," Jessie said coldly. "Meredith Baker."

Tom turned and gave the woman an angry look, but she put a hand up in defense.

"I'm sorry about that, Mr. Harrison, I really am. That's why I'm here. I knew Walker would want that last piece of the map, and I knew you guys would never give it to him, so I figured I could make a quick buck by getting a picture of it and selling it to him."

"You should be ashamed!" Benny scolded her, but Henry quickly hushed his little brother.

"You're right, I should. That's why I've been following all of you. After I sold the picture to Walker last night, I couldn't sleep, and it took me half the night to figure out why — I felt bad and was worried about what might happen to you kids. By the next morning I knew I had to do something about it."

Meredith reached into her pocket and pulled out a huge wad of cash with a rubber band around it. She threw it at Winston Walker, who caught it against his chest.

"You can have your money back, Mr. Walker," she said. "I don't want it. I know what people around this town think of me. I know they think I'm a little strange. But I've never committed a crime before, not until the other night." She turned to Tom and continued, "Mr. Harrison, I'm truly, truly sorry for what I did. Not only was it a crime, but it was just plain wrong. If you want to press charges against me, I'll understand."

All eyes turned to Tom, who appeared to be thinking over Meredith's offer. He began stroking his chin. "You know, I was thinking of putting together a nice color pamphlet advertising my inn, but the one thing I can't do is take a really good picture. You wouldn't happen to know any top-notch photographers, would you?"

Meredith stared blankly at Tom for a long moment. Then a broad smile spread across her face. "Actually, I think I do know someone. She's very good and I'm sure she'd do it for free."

Tom nodded slowly. "Is that right? Gee, she sounds perfect. Why don't you ask her to come to the house — through the *front door* this time — next Wednesday."

Meredith's smile grew even wider. "I sure will, Mr. Harrison. I sure will."

"Great," he replied. And with that, Meredith Baker turned and walked away, looking very happy.

Grandfather folded his arms and looked back at Winston Walker. "So, now, what were you saying before?" he asked sternly.

Walker said, "I was talking about Jack Ford and his mother, and how I'm going to buy a house for each of them."

"Oh, yes, of course. That's a very nice gesture, Mr. Walker," Grandfather told him, "but will you stick to your word?"

Winston Walker looked right into Grandfather Alden's eyes. "You better believe I will. I'll make things right with him, and with a whole lot of other people, too."

He climbed up out of the hole and brushed some of the dirt from his clothes. "Then I'm going to do something nice for you kids," he said.

"There's no reason for you to do that, Mr. Walker," Grandfather replied, but Winston Walker was already waving his hand.

"No, no, I insist. It'll be the right thing to help me get . . . well, get better, I guess."

For the first time since Grandfather met Winston Walker, he felt a little bit of fondness for him.

"Good for you, Winston," Grandfather said, patting him on the back.

"Yeah, good for you," Benny added with a smile.

Winston Walker smiled back at the youngest Alden and said, "Here — *Benny* — you can have this."

He thumbed John Finney's single gold coin into the air, and Benny caught it.

"Wow, thanks!" Benny said.

"You're welcome. And now, if you'll all excuse me, I've got a lot of work to do."

"Good luck," Jessie said.

"Thanks," Winston Walker replied, then turned and headed back down the sunlit nature trail. He reached the curve before the footbridge, followed it into the reeds, and was gone.

CHAPTER 10

Good News All Around

There were only two days of vacation left for the Aldens, and they were determined to spend them both at the beach.

Benny and Henry were playing in the ocean, running around and splashing each other, while Jessie and Violet lay on their towel, reading. Grandfather sat nearby in a folding chair, resting peacefully with his hands folded together on his chest. In the sand next to him was a little transistor radio broadcasting the day's baseball game.

There were hundreds of other sunbathers around, and for the first time none of them showed any interest in Benny. The great mystery of John Finney's treasure had finally been solved, and most people found the outcome more funny than anything else. It was yesterday's news. It had already been forgotten.

Tom came back from the boardwalk carrying a large cardboard box. "Food's here!" he called out. Benny turned quickly. He and Henry hurried over.

"Let's see, now . . . a hot dog for Henry, a hamburger for Violet, a cheeseburger for Jessie, some fries with each of those orders, and of course one of everything for Benny."

"Oh, boy, I'm starving!" Benny cried out excitedly, jumping up and down.

"What would you like first?" Tom asked.

"Ummm . . . the hot dog!" Benny replied.

Tom lifted one dog out of the box and handed it over. "There you go. Hey, James, your food is here."

Grandfather pushed up his sunglasses.

"Thanks, Tom. That should hit the spot right about now."

Everyone ate quietly while they listened to the game and watched other people playing in the waves.

When Grandfather was finished with his hamburger, he reached alongside his chair to get his copy of the day's newspaper.

"Did anyone see this?" he asked, displaying the front page. Right in the center was a picture of Winston Walker shaking hands with another man. Behind them was the old lighthouse where the town's historical society was located. The headline underneath the picture read, MILLIONAIRE TO DONATE PROFITS FROM BOOK DEAL TO LOCAL HISTORICAL SOCIETY.

Jessie said, "Book deal? What book deal? I didn't know he wrote a book."

"He hasn't yet," Grandfather told her, "but he's going to. According to the article, it's going to be called *Fool's Gold* and it's going to be partially about his worldwide search for John Finney's treasure. But mostly it's supposed to be about the foolishness of spending your whole life chasing nothing but money." Grandfather looked at the picture and shook his head. "He's been offered half a million dollars for the book. Even when he's not trying to make money, he still does."

"Some people are just like that," Tom said.

"Oh, and I forgot to mention that Jack Ford called this morning," said Grandfather.

"What did he say?" Benny asked eagerly. He and the other children had grown fond of him during his short visit.

Grandfather smiled. "It was hard to tell. He seemed a bit . . . in shock. He mumbled something about Winston Walker paying off his mother's house, and then buying her a new one. Then he bought one for Jack, too. They've both already been paid for. Jack didn't know what to say. He was speechless."

"It's wonderful that Winston Walker kept his word," Violet pointed out.

"It sure is," Tom told her.

He had not only kept his word about Jack Ford, but also about giving something to the Aldens, too. The morning after finding John Finney's box, a personal note from Winston came for the Aldens at Tom's house. It said simply that there were four brand-new bicycles waiting for the children at their favorite shop when they got back to Greenfield.

Grandfather laughed. "Jack wanted to know what made Winston change so quickly. I told him it was because of John Finney's treasure."

Benny looked confused. "But . . . there was no treasure."

"Oh, yes, there was," Grandfather said wisely. "Only it wasn't the kind of treasure Winston Walker was expecting."

Benny didn't quite understand what Grandfather meant, but Jessie did. "He found out what he had become, and he was given the chance to change it," she told everyone.

Her grandfather jabbed a finger at her.

"Exactly," he said proudly. "So it looks as though everything did turn out for the best."

"It sure did," Tom agreed.

Benny finished the last bite of his hamburger and looked back at the ocean. He really wanted to get into the water again, but he knew he shouldn't so soon after eating.

Then something caught his eye that made him jump up off his towel and run down there anyway — it was a bottle, bobbing back and forth in the foam.

He rushed in and grabbed it before the next wave could pull it back out. It was very, very old, much older than John Finney's . . . and was that a small piece of paper with something drawn on it inside?

No, Benny saw after his imagination calmed down. The bottle was no older than he was; it simply had been designed to *look* old. And the paper he saw wasn't on the inside. It was the bottle's label, pasted on the *other* side.

He brought it back to where everyone

was sitting so he could throw it in the trash when they left.

"Another treasure map, Benny?" Grandfather asked.

Benny shook his head. "No, but maybe that's okay."

He laughed then, and the others laughed with him.

Two days later the Aldens were back in Grandfather's station wagon, cruising north toward Greenfield, headed for home.

GERTRUDE CHANDLER WARNER discovered when she was teaching that many readers who like an exciting story could find no books that were both easy and fun to read. She decided to try to meet this need, and her first book, *The Boxcar Children*, quickly proved she had succeeded.

Miss Warner drew on her own experiences to write the mystery. As a child she spent hours watching trains go by on the tracks opposite her family home. She often dreamed about what it would be like to set up housekeeping in a caboose or freight car — the situation the Alden children find themselves in.

When Miss Warner received requests for more adventures involving Henry, Jessie, Violet, and Benny Alden, she began additional stories. In each, she chose a special setting and introduced unusual or eccentric characters who liked the unpredictable.

While the mystery element is central to each of Miss Warner's books, she never thought of them as strictly juvenile mysteries. She liked to stress the Aldens' independence and resourcefulness and their solid New England devotion to using up and making do. The Aldens go about most of their adventures with as little adult supervision as possible — something else that delights young readers.

Miss Warner lived in Putnam, Connecticut, until her death in 1979. During her lifetime, she received hundreds of letters from girls and boys telling her how much they liked her books.